The
MOUNT
RUSHMORE
Face That
Couldn't See

by
Steve Brezenoff

illustrated by
Marcos Calo

STONE ARCH BOOKS
a capstone imprint

r Samantha Archer,

Field Trip Mysteries are published by Stone Arch Books
A Capstone Imprint
1710 Roe Crest Drive
North Mankato, Minnesota 56003
www.capstonepub.com

Library of Congress Cataloging-in-Publication Data
Brezenoff, Steven.
The Mount Rushmore face that couldn't see / by Steve
Brezenoff ; illustrated by Marcos Calo.
p. cm. -- (Field trip mysteries)
ISBN 978-1-4342-3787-3 (library binding) -- ISBN 978-1-4342-
4199-3 (pbk.)
1. School field trips--Juvenile fiction. 2. Vandalism-
-Juvenile fiction. 3. Mount Rushmore National Memorial
(S.D.)--Juvenile fiction. [1. School field trips--Fiction.
2. Vandalism--Fiction. 3. Mount Rushmore National Memorial
(S.D.)--Fiction. 4. Mystery and detective stories.] I. Calo,
Marcos, ill. II. Title. III. Title: Mount Rushmore face that
could not see. IV. Series: Brezenoff, Steven. Field trip
mysteries.

813.6--dc23

PZ7.B7576Mou 2012

Graphic Designer: Kay Fraser

Summary: When Catalina "Cat" Duran and her
friends in the History Club arrive at Mount
Rushmore on a school trip, they find that
someone is playing dangerous tricks and trying
to drive people away from the park.

Printed in the United States of America in
Stevens Point, Wisconsin.
032012   006678WZF12

TABLE OF CONTENTS

Catalina Duran

A.K.A: Cat

D.O.B: February 15th

POSITION: 6th Grade

INTERESTS:

Animals, being "green", field trips

KNOWN ASSOCIATES:

Archer, Samantha; Garrison, Edward;
and Shoo, James. *Are these students spending too much time together?*

NOTES:

Catalina is well liked by most of
her teachers and fellow students.
Sounds like a troublemaker.

A SUMMER TRIP

One thing I'll always remember about **Mount Rushmore:** It's far.

It's far from everything else in the world, I think.

My best friends and I went with the rest of the History Club on a special summer trip. The bus ride was long. And it was hot.

The bus's air conditioner wasn't working, so all the windows were as far open as they'd go.

"Cat," said Samantha, better known as Sam. She was sitting next to me in the back row of the bus. Her voice was quiet and dry. "Pass me the bottle of water, please."

I nodded slowly and reached into my tote bag. "It's almost empty," I said. I handed it to Sam. "Don't finish it. It's the last water we have."

Sam frowned as she unscrewed the cap. She took a short sip.

"Thanks," she said. She could barely get the words out.

I leaned my head against the window, letting the warm summer air blow across my face a little. It didn't help much, but it was better than nothing.

"It's . . . so . . . hot," I said.

Sam tried to nod. Her mouth fell open and she panted. Then she closed her eyes and collapsed against my shoulder.

"Stop being such drama queens!" Gum said. He and Egg were sitting across the aisle, watching me and Sam.

Egg snapped a picture of Sam playing dead. Then we all busted up laughing.

"Okay, future historians," said Ms. Juniper, the gym teacher and the faculty advisor of the History Club. She was in the front of the bus, standing carefully in the aisle, holding on to the back of a seat.

She also had a whistle around her neck. She always had a whistle around her neck. "We'll be arriving shortly," she said.

Everyone cheered, except Anton Gutman. He stood up and shouted, "No problem! After all, Egg does everything shortly." Then he cracked up.

No one else laughed. Not even his two thug friends. "Get it?" Anton said through his laughter. "Because he's short?"

Ms. Juniper blew her whistle. Even at the back of the bus, I had to slap my hands over my ears. That's how loud Ms. Juniper's whistle was.

Anton was sitting right next to Ms. Juniper. She liked to keep him close where he couldn't cause trouble. The whistle was close to his ear, and he actually fell over.

"That's enough of that, Anton," Ms. Juniper said. "You are on this trip because your grade in history was beyond terrible. One more mean word out of you, my friend, and you'll spend the rest of your life in the sixth grade."

She sighed. "Now, as I was saying," she went on, "we're nearly there. As we come around the next bend, you can look at the windows on the right side of the bus. What you'll see is pretty amazing."

Everyone strained and leaned to see out the windows as we came around a bend, going uphill.

I had one of the best seats on the bus. In front of us was a small grove of evergreen trees and then a sloping field of rocks. The bus slowed down till it was barely rolling.

At the top of the field of rocks, past a few more pine trees, was an amazing sight: Mount Rushmore.

Sam said, "Whoa."

Gum gave a low whistle.

Egg snapped photo after photo.

I smiled.

There was the most famous sculpture and the most famous mountain in the United States. The faces of George Washington, Thomas Jefferson, Theodore Roosevelt, and Abraham Lincoln, four of the country's greatest presidents. The faces were carved right into the side of the mountain, a hundred times larger than life.

The whole History Club was awed. We'd all been excited for this trip, and now that we were here . . . wow.

Except Anton, of course. He just laughed. "Hey," he said, pointing out the window, "the guy on the right has a big booger on his face."

Sam stood up in her seat. She leaned far forward and shouted at Anton, "That's Abe Lincoln, you dummy."

"Everyone sit down!" Ms. Juniper said. Then the bus started on again, back down the hill toward the park's main entrance.

"Whatever," Anton said. He smiled at his goon friends. "Whoever that guy is, he has a big booger on his face."

FIRST ACTIVITY

The only bad thing about getting the back seat (the best seat) on the bus is that you're always the last person off the bus. That day, with the temperature about a million degrees, waiting to get off the bus was not easy.

By the time Sam and I finally tumbled off the bus, we could hardly breathe. But the air outside in the Mount Rushmore National Memorial park was much cooler. It even smelled nice — like pine trees and fresh-cut grass.

"We have two very busy days ahead of us, gang," Ms. Juniper said. "Everyone get your gear and your lunches from the bus's cargo hold. We'll eat quickly, then start our adventures!"

* * *

Unpacking and eating didn't take long. We'd all been told to pack light. I'd brought a change of clothes, a notebook, and a sleeping bag, plus one lunch and toothbrushes and stuff, of course. We sat down for lunch at some picnic tables next to the parking lot. By then we were all completely starving.

Just as I was swallowing the last bite of my cheese and cucumber and tomato sandwich, Egg started clicking his camera like crazy.

It was weird. Not Egg taking photos. He takes photos all the time.

The weird thing was he was pointing the camera at the parking lot behind me.

"Um, Egg?" I said. "The monument is over there."

Egg snapped a couple more times. "I know," he said. "I'm not taking pictures of the monument right now. Look."

A group of high-school-age kids was gathered right in the middle of the parking lot. Some of them were carrying signs, but from where we were, I couldn't read them.

"What do you suppose they're doing?" Sam asked.

Gum wasn't impressed. He went back to eating his baloney sandwich. "Who knows," he said through a mouthful of food. "People will protest anything. Remember when Cat protested at the zoo?"

"Those animals were cooped up in tiny, tiny cages!" I replied, annoyed.

Sam raised her hand. "Ms. Juniper," she said. "Why are those people here?" She pointed toward the group in the parking lot.

Ms. Juniper glanced up from her sandwich. "Them?" she said. She squinted, trying to get a look at their signs. "I don't know."

A park security guard strolled by. "They're Lakota kids," he said. "There are several Lakota reservations here in South Dakota."

"What are they
protesting?" I asked.

"It's complicated," the guard said. "The short answer is that they think this land and this mountain are Lakota property." Someone called for the guard, and he jogged off.

"Everyone finish up," Ms. Juniper said. She gave a couple of short blows on her whistle. "It's time for our first activity. Who's ready for the Ranger Walk?"

It sounds dorky, but after being cooped up on that hot bus, we actually cheered. So we were all disappointed when that security guard came running back to the picnic area.

"The Ranger Walk is off!" the guard was shouting. "Ranger Harrison is missing!"

CHAPTER THREE

THE MISSING RANGER

"Missing?" Ms. Juniper said. "Doesn't the ranger live on the park grounds?"

The guard nodded. "Yes," he said. "He shares a cabin with his daughter. I'm heading over to his cabin now. The caretaker will meet me there."

Sam whispered, "Get up. We have to follow the guard so we can see what's going on."

The four of us stayed well behind the guard as he jogged across the grounds. He didn't notice us. At the cabin, we hid among some bushes around the corner from the front door.

Ranger Harrison's house was a small log cabin among a few tall pines. Standing on the front porch was an old man in a brown shirt and pants. "I'm ready to open the door, if you need me to," the old man said.

The guard nodded. Then he banged on the door. "Ranger Harrison," the guard shouted through the door. "Are you in there?"

There was no answer. My friends and I quietly came around the corner. The guard patted the old man on the back.

"Go ahead," the guard said. "Open the door."

The old man pulled a long chain from his pocket. Then he unlocked the door and pushed it open.

"Thanks, Herman," the guard said. They walked into the cabin.

A second later, Sam crept in after them. Egg, Gum, and I had no choice but to go in too.

"Harrison?" the guard called. "Are you in here?"

No response. The guard walked into the back hallway. "Hello?" he said.

"Hey," Egg whispered close to my ear, "where did the old guy go?"

An instant later, a hand gripped my shoulder. The caretaker snapped, "What are you kids doing?"

Egg and I spun to face the caretaker. "You kids shouldn't be here," he said. "Why aren't you with your class?"

"We —," Sam started to say.

The guard cut her off. "Ranger Harrison!" he shouted. He ran through the bedroom door.

My friends and I ran in behind him. A man wearing striped green pajamas was tied to the bed. A red and white bandanna was tied over his mouth. His eyes were wide with fear.

ALL TIED UP

"Who did this to you?" the guard said after he pulled the bandanna from the ranger's mouth.

"I don't know," the ranger said. He gasped and breathed heavily and quickly. "Please, untie me."

We ran to the bed to help.

"What are you doing?" the guard said. "This is a crime scene."

"We're detectives," Sam said. "Honorary ones, anyway."

The guard just stood there, looking shocked, as we untied the ranger.

"Didn't you see the culprit, sir?" Sam asked.

"Whoever it was," Ranger Harrison said, shrugging, "he tied me up while I was still asleep." He got up from the bed and stretched his arms. "That feels much better," he said. "Thanks."

"I'll have to call the police," the guard said. He left the room as he pulled out his walkie-talkie.

"Doesn't your daughter live here too?" I asked the ranger. "Maybe she saw something."

"She always leaves the house very early," the ranger said. "She likes to take a hike at sunrise. Then she helps at the gift shop."

Egg snapped a few photos of the bedroom. "Good idea," Sam said, nodding. "It's super important to take pictures of the crime scene."

"Wow, you kids really are detectives, huh?" the ranger asked.

"We solve crimes all the time," Gum said.

The ranger looked around the room. His eyes fell on a gold watch on the dresser. Then he glanced at his laptop computer on a desk in the corner. Finally, he looked at his cell phone, which was on the night stand next to his bed.

"I don't get it," the ranger said. "Whoever did this, they didn't steal anything. Nothing at all."

Sam frowned. But before I could ask her what she was thinking, the ranger cleared his throat.

"Well, kids," he said, "it's been a pleasure to meet you, but I have a Ranger Walk to lead, so I better get into uniform. If you'll excuse me?"

He led us toward the cabin's door. The caretaker followed us out and closed the door behind us.

The Ranger Walk was pretty interesting. Ranger Harrison taught us all about the natural history of the mountain, and he also told us about who used to live there.

It turned out the protestors in the parking lot were kind of right. The Lakota people had lived there for a long time before the United States even existed. Ranger Harrison said they called the mountain Six Grandfathers. It was renamed "Mount Rushmore" in the 1800s.

Of course, Sam wouldn't let me listen too closely to Ranger Harrison. She was too busy thinking about why he'd been tied up in his cabin.

"What I don't get," Sam said, "is why anyone would tie up the ranger if they didn't want to rob him."

"I can think of one reason I would have tied up that ranger," Gum said. "So my feet wouldn't hurt."

"What are you talking about?" Sam asked. "Your feet hurt because we've been hiking."

"Exactly," Gum said. "And if the ranger had stayed tied up in his bed, we wouldn't be hiking. So my feet wouldn't hurt."

Sam smiled. "I get it," she said. "Whoever tied up that ranger might have been trying to stop him from leading this hike."

"But why?" I said.

"That," Sam said, winking at me, "is the question."

"Our next activity is in one hour," Ms. Juniper said when the hike was over. "Stay nearby."

Ranger Harrison said goodbye to us. Then he walked down to the parking lot. A police car was there. The ranger went over to the officers.

"Should we go listen in?" Egg said.

Sam nodded. "You go ahead," she said. "Don't get too close. Cat and I will find the ranger's daughter at the gift shop."

Egg nodded.

Gum said, "I have to spy with Egg? I wanted to go to the gift shop!"

"There'll be time for both," I said.

Sam and I waved as Egg and Gum walked off. Then she and I went into the gift shop.

Most of the History Club was already inside. A woman about my mom's age was on a stool behind the counter.

"I don't think that's Ranger Harrison's daughter," I whispered to Sam.

We walked around the store. Finally, in the back corner, we found a girl standing on a stool, dusting a shelf full of models of Mount Rushmore.

"Hello," I said.

The girl turned around and looked down at me and Sam. I smiled at her. "Hi," she said. "Do you need help finding something?"

"We were looking for you, actually," Sam said.

"Um, me?" she said. Her eyes darted around the store. She looked like maybe she needed a way to escape.

But there was something else in her eyes, too. I couldn't quite put my finger on it.

"You are Ranger Harrison's daughter, right?" Sam asked.

"Yup," the girl said, "I'm Ruthie Harrison."

"Is your father okay?" I asked. "We . . . heard about what happened this morning."

"Oh," the girl said. "Yes, he's fine. Thanks. Didn't he just lead your tour?"

My face got hot. Of course he was okay. I felt stupid for asking.

"Still," Sam said quickly, "it was probably pretty upsetting for him to be tied up like that."

The girl shrugged. "I guess so," she said. "Listen, I'm supposed to be working, not standing around chatting. I'll see you."

Ruthie walked off, carrying her duster, and disappeared into the gift shop's back room.

THE STUDIO

Our next field trip activity was in the Sculptor's Studio. Ms. Juniper led the way. "This should be very interesting," she said. "Especially for you kids who are also in the Art Club."

It was like a mini-museum. There were sculptor's tools and little models of the monument itself. Plus, since the monument was so big, some of the tools were not your typical sculptor's tools. There were climbing gear, huge picks, and a small version of the monument that took up a lot of the room.

"Look at this!" Egg said. He was over by the window, snapping photos.

The view of the monument was amazing. Gum and I hurried over to look, but Sam grabbed my wrist.

"Guys," she hissed. "Look!"

She was pointing at a piece of equipment behind Egg. It was like a cylinder, with a crank on each side. It was behind a rope and obviously hadn't been touched in years. But now it was turning all on its own. Everyone gasped.

Then a low voice boomed from the copy of the monument. "Get out!" it said.

Ms. Juniper screamed. I was pretty scared too. Sam tried to get closer, of course, but the old caretaker shoved his way through the crowd.

"Out of the way," he snapped. "Move aside." He looked up at the sculpture. "Which of 'em said it?" he said.

"Huh?" Sam said.

"Which president?" the caretaker asked. "Did their lips move?"

"Are you serious?" Sam asked.

The caretaker nodded. Then he looked at the cylinder. The cranks still turned.

"It's the ghosts," the man said. "The ghosts of the presidents. Everyone out! Now! Before they get us!"

"You heard him," Ms. Juniper said. "Everyone out."

We started moving toward the exit, but something was shoving the crowd from the other side.

"We want to see the ghost," a voice said.

"You haven't paid," said the woman at the door. "You have to pay the entrance fee to enter the studio."

The crowd got shoved back against me and my friends, and soon a bunch of the protestors were in the studio.

One of them stood in the middle of the room. He watched the cylinder as the crank slowed and then stopped.

"This was not the ghost of a president," the protester said. "What reason would these men have to return?"

He walked across the floor. The crowd watched him as he paced the room.

"This ghost," the protester finally went on, "was a Lakota spirit. You have to listen to the spirit's warning and leave this Lakota land at once."

Just then, several security guards came in. "Everyone out, now," one of them said. "And you protestors, if you don't leave right away, you'll be taken to the police station for entering without paying the fee."

The crowd and the protestors moved toward the exit. "I wonder if this haunting is related to Ranger Harrison being tied to his bed," Sam whispered. Egg, Gum, and I leaned in closer as we walked slowly for the door.

"They both sound like nasty pranks," Gum said.

"I know who you're thinking about," Egg said. "Anton Gutman."

"I'm not convinced it's that simple," Sam said.

The crowd finally thinned out enough so we could get outside into the open air.

"So what should we do?" I asked. "Start asking questions?"

"I'll interrogate Anton," Gum said.

Sam shook her head. "Not yet," she said. "We need to start with the scene of the crime. We're going back into the studio."

CHAPTER SEVEN

SNEAKING IN

"I don't think that's going to be so easy," Egg said.

The four of us were standing about ten yards from the entrance to the art studio. The rest of the History Club was standing around chatting. But up at the studio's entrance, four security guards were blocking the door.

"We'll have to go around back," Sam said. "There must be another way in."

We started toward the back of the building. To avoid being seen, we walked in a very wide circle, so it took much longer than it would have if the guards hadn't been there. Of course, if the guards hadn't been there, we could have just walked right in through the front door.

"We don't even know if there is a door back there," Gum pointed out. "Maybe we should turn back."

"Don't be ridiculous," Sam said. "How will we solve this mystery if we don't investigate?"

"I don't see any door," Egg said.

He was right. I just saw that big window — the one Egg had been taking photos through. But Sam spotted something else.

"Shh," she said. She crouched down behind a pine tree.

The rest of us followed her lead. "I saw someone," Sam said. "Someone prowling around behind the building."

We all stayed quiet. "There," Gum whispered. "Behind those bushes." There was a figure there, skulking around in the plants behind the studio.

"I can't tell who it is," Sam said.

"Give me a second," Egg said. He pushed a button on his camera. "I see him now."

He snapped about ten photos. Then he turned around the camera and held up the display for us to see: it was the caretaker.

Egg clicked through the pictures he'd taken. On the last one, the caretaker was looking right at the camera.

"Uh-oh," Egg said. "He saw us!"

We all turned and looked at the building. The caretaker was walking right toward us.

Sam jumped to her feet and shouted, "Run!"

We sprinted and dodged between trees, galloping down the hill toward the rest of the History Club.

As he gasped for breath, Egg said, "I don't think he can catch us."

"Keep running," Sam said. She led us behind a tall, thick bush. I guess she wanted to hide. Instead, someone jumped out at us, and we screamed.

"Anton!" I shouted. Then I slapped him on the arm.

It didn't hurt him. I just couldn't help myself.

Anton couldn't stop laughing. He looked like was practically in pain, the way he was bent over and holding his stomach.

"You should have seen your faces," Anton said. He wiped some tears of laughter from his eyes.

"Whatever, Anton," Gum said. "So you startled us a little. Big deal."

"Anyway," Anton said, still smiling, "Ms. Jupiter —"

"It's Juniper," I said.

Anton ignored me. "She sent me up here to get you dorks," he said. "We're supposed to get our gear and hike to the campsite now." Then he ran off down the hill again. He laughed the whole way.

"He can't ruin my mood," Egg said. He held up his camera and pointed at the display screen. "This was the easiest mystery we've ever had. The caretaker did it, and I have the proof right here."

CHAPTER EIGHT

CAMPSITE

The hike to the campsite was much more pleasant than the Ranger Walk had been. It was a nice flat trail, for one thing. For another, the sun was nice and low. It was very refreshing.

"The campsite is just over this ridge," Ms. Juniper said. Just as the sun set in front of us, we reached a large clearing in the pine forest.

It was beautiful. Gum unrolled his sleeping bag and lay down. Sam immediately pulled out a deck of cards and started shuffling. Egg snapped lots of photos of the sunset.

I knew none of those pictures would do the scene justice, though. It was too beautiful for a camera. So I sat down on a rock in the middle of the clearing and tried to enjoy it.

Ms. Juniper and a few of the kids got a campfire going. Then she passed out hot dogs and veggie dogs to roast. It wasn't the tastiest meal I'd ever had, but it was a lot of fun.

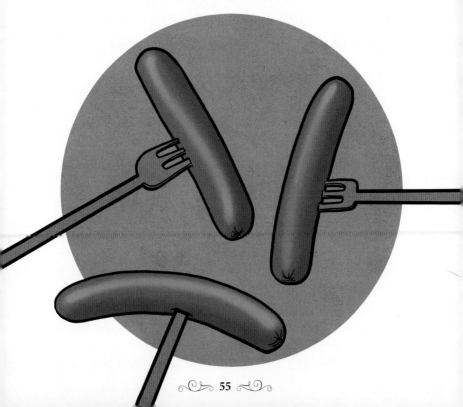

"This is an amazing field trip," I said. "I can't wait to fall asleep staring up at that sky. I've never seen so many stars!"

"Don't get too comfy," said Anton. He crouched down next to me. "We might have to run if a cougar comes to eat us."

"Very funny," Sam said. She didn't even look up from her card game. "Now buzz off."

Anton walked off. We could hear him laughing as he wandered toward his sleeping bag. He'd set up with his thug friends, just inside the tree line.

I climbed into my sleeping bag—it's got a cozy flannel lining inside, and pictures of cats, of course. Lying on my back, I stared up at the sky. The stars were so bright. I decided that when this trip was over, I'd buy ten packs of glow-in-the-dark stars to hang on the ceiling of my bedroom.

I was completely relaxed and happy. I probably would have fallen asleep smiling.

But then there was a flash of light not far away, just a few feet into the forest. Then a low voice, just like the one we'd heard at the studio, boomed through the cool night air: "Go home! We are the spirits of the Lakota people. Go home!"

Everyone screamed this time, except Sam. Sam isn't really scared of anything. Egg calmed down quickly. He and Gum asked me if I was okay.

"I think so," I said, looking around the area. "My heart is going a mile a minute, though."

Gum sat next to me. Egg grabbed his camera and took lots of pictures with the flash. As the flash went off and sent bright light into the woods, we could just see people moving around.

"I see them!" Sam said. She darted into the woods.

The low voice screamed, like it was scared or in pain. There was another flash of light, but this time it wasn't from Egg's camera.

"What was that?" I hissed.

Gum shook his head and said, "I don't know."

Then the light flickered a little. Something crackled. Suddenly there was a little orange explosion. Then the woods were lit up in an orange glow. Something in those woods was on fire.

FIRE!

Sam and Ms. Juniper were the only ones from the History Club who didn't lose it. "Toss me a blanket," Sam shouted. "A heavy one."

Ms. Juniper nodded. She found a dark heavy blanket. She rolled it up and tossed it to Sam.

Sam darted into the woods. In seconds, the orange light died down and was gone.

Egg, Gum, and I ran over to Sam. "What started this fire?" I asked.

Gum chuckled. "This might sound crazy," he said, "but Anton and his two dork friends were setting up their camp right near here."

"Normally, I'd be happy to see Anton and his goons in trouble," Sam said. She stood up and dusted herself off. "But look at this."

She was holding a long cable. The end of it was frayed. Bare wires stuck out in every direction. "Here's your fire starter," Sam said.

"An electrical cable?" Gum said. He reached out to grab it.

"Careful!" Sam said, pulling it away. "It might be alive still."

Gum jumped back. "Okay then," he said. "But I don't think Lakota ghosts usually use electricity. It might still have been Anton."

"No," Sam said. "I think I know who put this here. And it wasn't Anton. Follow me."

Egg, Gum, and I followed as Sam kept her hands on the wire. She followed its trail as it wound under the leaves and twigs on the forest floor.

The cable led right back toward our campsite. Sam suddenly stopped just inside the trees. "Aha!" she said.

We gathered around. Ms. Juniper stood right behind and peeked over my head. "What is it?" she asked.

Sam put her hands on her hips. "It's just what I thought," she said. "A speaker."

We all woke up a little after sunrise. Even those of us who could have slept in bright daylight woke up from the heat.

"Everyone up!" Ms. Juniper said. "Pack up your gear. We'll put everything back on the bus before breakfast."

"On the bus?" I repeated. "Is the field trip over already?"

"It can't be," Egg whispered to me. "We haven't caught the culprit yet!"

Sam stroked her chin. "I think we're close," she said.

Egg and I squinted at our friend. She didn't say another word.

"Not to worry, Cat," Ms. Juniper said. "We've saved the best for last. After breakfast, we'll take a tour of the Lakota Heritage Village."

After we'd all finished eating, Ms. Juniper blew her whistle. "Everyone," she said, "this is Ranger Betty."

Ranger Betty was a short lady with dark hair, wearing tan ranger pants and a blue ranger shirt. She also had on a tan hat with a big brim. "Hi, kids," she said. "Ready for your tour?"

Ranger Betty led us up a trail to the heritage village. It was set up to look just like a real Native American village. There were teepees and everything.

"This heritage village is the newest exhibit at Mount Rushmore," Ranger Betty told us. "It was set up to show how the Lakota, Dakota, and Nakota nations lived before the United States began its growth to the west."

Egg was snapping loads of photos. I ran over to a teepee. "Get a picture of me!" I called. "For my parents."

My family is from Mexico. That means we have a lot of Native American blood in our veins. I knew my parents would have loved to visit this place.

Before Egg could take a single shot, though, there was a great boom from the hill at the top of the village.

We all watched the woods. A great cloud of smoke came shooting down the mountain.

There was another loud boom, and then that voice – the same deep, deep voice – shouted, "Go home!"

HOME!

Everyone screamed. Only my friends and I, and Ms. Juniper, stayed calm.

Sam jogged to the back of one of the teepees. I followed as she got down on her knees and scraped around in the dirt. Very carefully, she pinched at a tiny spot of ground. Then she lifted her fingers, still pinched together. She smiled.

I leaned down and squinted at Sam's fingers. Then I saw it. "Fishing line!" I said.

Sam nodded. "This is how some of these hauntings are happening," she said.

"What about the voice?" I asked.

Sam got up and took my hand. "Come on," she said.

We hurried down to the rest of the History Club. "Ms. Juniper," Sam called out. "Get one of the security guards."

"Why?" the teacher asked.

"Sam solved the crimes," I said. "Uh, I think."

Ms. Juniper, a park guard, and Ranger Harrison gathered around me and the rest of the field-trip mystery solvers.

Sam got right to it. "All right, everybody. I know who's been causing all the trouble," she said.

Egg raised his hand. "It's those protestors," he said. "Right? They have the motive. Plus, it makes sense they'd pretend to be Lakota spirits, since they speak for some of the Lakota nation."

"That does make sense," Sam said, "but they don't have the opportunity."

"That's right," I said. "They couldn't have gotten into Ranger Harrison's house."

"Or the studio," Gum pointed out. "You all saw how the security team reacted when they went inside."

"They didn't pay," the park guard said.

"Only one person has motive and opportunity," Sam said. "The caretaker."

Ranger Harrison and the park guard looked shocked.

"Think about it," Sam said. She started pacing, like an old-time detective. Sam loved all those old movies. "The caretaker has a set of keys that opens every door in the park."

"That's true," the park guard said.

"But what motive does he have?" Egg said.

"He's a grump," Sam said. "You saw how he looked at us, and how he talked to us. He doesn't like kids. He wants us out of here. And he doesn't want any more groups showing up, either."

That got me thinking about kids.

There was one kid at the park who wasn't here with a class trip. She'd never be going anywhere.

"This makes sense," the park guard said. He reached for his walkie-talkie. "I'll give the order to arrest the caretaker at once."

"Wait!" I said. "It wasn't the caretaker."

Sam looked at me, her eyes wide.

"Then who do you think it was, Cat?" Egg said.

I didn't answer right away. I looked over his shoulder and saw a girl peeking out from behind a teepee.

"There's one person who has the best motive of all," I said, looking right at the girl. She looked back at me. Now I knew what I'd seen in her eyes before, at the gift shop. "Homesickness."

"I just wanted to go home," Ruthie Harrison said. She sat with her father on a bench near the entrance to the gift shop.

Ranger Harrison cleared his throat and tried to smile. He was obviously upset and embarrassed. "I thought you were having fun here, Ruthie," he said.

Ruthie shrugged. "It was fun at first," she said. "But now I miss home. I miss the city, and all my friends."

Ranger Harrison sighed. "I wish you'd told me," he said.

"I don't get it," Egg said. "Why did you go all this trouble? Why make it look like Lakota ghosts?"

"Yeah," Gum said. "You didn't think you'd fool anyone, did you?"

Ruthie shook her head. "I wanted the guards to think the protestors were causing the trouble," she said. "I figured that way I could get the park shut down, and the protestors would get blamed."

"But why did you tie me up?" Ranger Harrison asked. "That was you, wasn't it?"

Ruthie looked at her hands in her lap. She nodded, and a tear fell. "I figured if you were late to the tour," she said, "you'd get fired. Then we'd have to go back to the city."

"But you left me there," Ranger Harrison said. "Someone was bound to find me."

"I was coming back for you!" Ruthie said. "But when I got to the house, the guard was already banging on the door. I ran."

The ranger looked at his daughter for a long time. Then he put his arms around her. "I'm sorry, Ruthie," he said. "I didn't know how much you missed home."

I decided Ruthie and her dad should have some privacy, so I grabbed Sam's elbow and pulled her away. Then I hissed at Gum and Egg to come too. The four of us walked down the hill toward the parking lot.

"So how did you figure out it was Ruthie?" Sam asked. "I was so sure it was the caretaker."

"The ghost gave it away," I said. "It always said 'Go home,' and that reminded me of Ruthie. I realized how homesick she seemed when we saw her at the gift shop."

Sam nodded. Then she patted me on the back. "Nice job," she said.

"Do you think Ruthie will get in big trouble?" Egg asked.

"If I pulled a stunt like that," Gum said, "I'd be grounded for a hundred years."

"Look on the bright side, then," I said. "If she's grounded, she'll have to stay in her house."

"Why is that the bright side?" Sam asked.

I laughed. "Well," I said, "she sure won't be homesick anymore!"

literary news

MYSTERIOUS WRITER REVEALED!

Steve Brezenoff lives in St. Paul, Minnesota, with his wife, Beth, their son, Sam, and their small, smelly dog, Harry. Besides writing books, he enjoys playing video games, riding his bicycle, and helping middle-school students work on their writing skills. Steve's ideas almost always come to him in his dreams, so he does his best writing in his pajamas.

arts & entertainment

ARTIST IS KEY TO SOLVING MYSTERY, SAY POLICE

Marcos Calo lives happily in A Coruña, Spain, with his wife, Patricia (who is also an illustrator), and their daughter, Claudia. When Marcos and Patricia aren't drawing, they like to go on long walks by the sea. They also watch a lot of films and eat Nutella sandwiches. Yum!

A Detective's Dictionary

awed (AWD)—amazed

crank (KRANGK)—a handle that makes something turn

culprit (KUHL-prit)—a person who has done something wrong

cylinder (SIL-uhn-dur)—a shape with flat, circular ends and sides shaped like the outside of a tube

historian (hiss-TOR-ee-uhn)—someone who studies history

honorary (ON-uh-rer-ee)—given as an honor without the usual requirements

interrogate (in-TER-uh-gate)—ask many questions

investigate (in-VESS-tuh-gate)—find out as much as possible about something

monument (MON-yuh-muhnt)—a statue or building, etc., that is meant to remind people of a person or event

motive (MOH-tiv)—a reason for doing something

protest (PROH-test)—a demonstration against something

ranger (RAYN-jur)—someone in charge of a park or forest

reservation (rez-ur-VAY-shuhn)—an area of land set aside by the government for a special purpose

Catalina Duran

Sixth Grade

A

Mount Rushmore

Mount Rushmore is a monument located near Keystone, South Dakota. It is a famous tourist destination because of the faces of four United States Presidents carved into the mountain – George Washington, Thomas Jefferson, Abraham Lincoln, and Teddy Roosevelt – but the massive sculpture has more stories than most people know.

Mount Rushmore was originally known to the Lakota people as Six Grandfathers. It is located on land that originally belonged to the Lakota tribe.

The land was seized by the United States after the Great Sioux War of 1876. The land is controversial among some groups because of this reason. Many people say it should be returned to the Native American tribe that once owned it.

In 1927, construction began on the four faces. It took four years and more than four hundred workers to sculpt the four faces on the side of Mount Rushmore. The whole project cost almost one million dollars to complete.

Cat – Great essay. I hope you enjoyed Mount Rushmore, and I appreciate knowing more about its history!

.. Ms. J.

FURTHER INVESTIGATIONS

CASE #FTM15CDMR

1. In this book, my class went on a field trip. What field trips have you gone on? Which one was your favorite, and why?

2. If you went on a field trip to Mount Rushmore, what would you be most excited to see? Talk about your answer.

3. Who else could have been a suspect in this mystery?

IN YOUR OWN DETECTIVE'S NOTEBOOK . . .

1. Write about a time you were homesick. What happened? How did you deal with it?

2. Sam, Cat, Gum, and Egg are best friends. Write about your best friend.

3. This book is a mystery story. Write your own mystery story!

FIELD TRIP MYSTERIES

THEY SOLVE CRIMES, CATCH CROOKS, CRACK CODES, ...AND RIDE THE BUS BACK TO SCHOOL AFTERWARD.

Meet Egg, Gum, Sam, and Cat. Four sixth-grade detectives and best friends. Wherever field trips take them, mysteries aren't far behind!

FIELD TRIP MYSTERIES

The
GRAND CANYON
Burros That Broke

by Steve Brezenoff   Illustrated by Marcos Calo

FIELD TRIP MYSTERIES

The
Mount
RUSHMORE
Face That
Couldn't See

by Steve Brezenoff   Illustrated by Marcos Calo

FIELD TRIP MYSTERIES

The
YELLOWSTONE
Kidnapping That Wasn't

by Steve Brezenoff   Illustrated by Marcos Calo

FIELD TRIP MYSTERIES

The
EVERGLADES
Poacher Who Pretended

by Steve Brezenoff   Illustrated by Marcos Calo

4
New
Mysteries

WAIT!
DON'T close the book!
There's MORE!
FIND MORE:
games
puzzles
heroes
villains
authors
illustrators at...
www.
capstonekids
.com
Still want MORE?
Find cool websites and more books like this one at www.Facthound.com.
Just type in the Book ID: 9781434237873 and you're ready to go!